The Tiger-Skin Rug

For Ruby

Bloomsbury Publishing, London, New Delhi, New York and Sydney

Hardback edition first published by Bloomsbury Publishing Plc in 2011
Paperback edition first published by Bloomsbury Publishing Plc in 2011

Bloomsbury Publishing Plc, 50 Bedford Square, London, WC1B 3DP

First published in Great Britain in 1979 by Faber and Faber Limited

Text and illustrations copyright © Gerald Rose 1979
The moral right of the author/illustrator has been asserted

A CIP catalogue record of this book is available from the British Library

Hardback ISBN 978 1 4088 1302 7

1 3 5 7 9 10 8 6 4 2

Paperback ISBN 978 1 4088 1303 4

3 5 7 9 10 8 6 4

Printed and bound in China

www.bloomsbury.com

The Tiger-Skin Rug

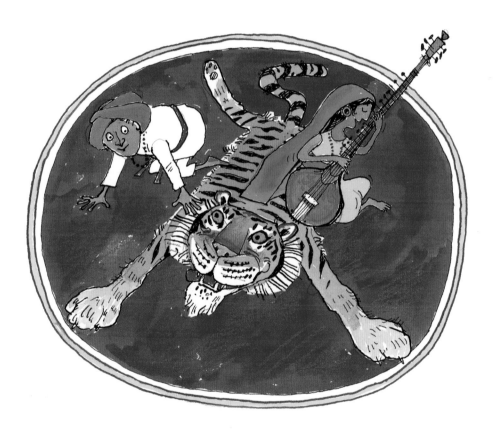

Gerald Rose

BLOOMSBURY

LONDON NEW DELHI NEW YORK SYDNEY

THERE WAS ONCE A VERY THIN TIGER, who lived on the edge of the jungle. He was sad and thin because he was getting old and food was difficult to catch. The monkeys threw nuts at him and called him names.

At night he would gaze at the Rajah's palace and sometimes he would look in the windows as the Rajah and his family ate their food in warmth and comfort. He wished that he could join their friendly company.

One day he was watching a servant beating the rugs in the palace gardens. One of the rugs was a tiger-skin. The tiger had an idea. While the servant's back was turned he jumped over the wall, took down the old tiger-skin rug, hid it under a bush and draped himself over the line.

The servant continued with his beating and beat poor Tiger even harder than the rest of the rugs, because he looked so dusty and moth-eaten.

Finally, when there was not a speck of dust left, the servant carried all the rugs back into the palace and spread them about in their correct places.

Tiger was put in the dining hall.
Soon the Rajah and his family came in to have their
evening meal. They laughed and ate and talked and

Tiger was glad to be in their company. They did not notice him, for he looked thin and moth-eaten, just like the old tiger-skin rug which they were used to.

After the meal, when they had all left the room, Tiger jumped up and finished all the scraps. Then he drank some tea and lay down for a good night's sleep. This was a wonderful life and he was determined not

to spoil it. Every day he enjoyed the family's company. Every evening he finished the scraps and drank some tea . . . but he was careful to keep very still whenever anyone came into the room.

At first nobody suspected that he was not the real tiger-skin rug, because he was so thin and looked so moth-eaten. The Rajah would play and frighten the children with him. The children would pretend he was a real live tiger.

But Tiger was worried, because he knew that he was not as thin as he used to be, or as moth-eaten.

One day the Rajah said, 'How strange – the old tiger-skin rug has improved with age. But it really is beginning to smell. If it cannot be cleaned it will have to go.'

The following day the tiger was taken out into the garden and scrubbed with an old broom. The soap made his eyes sting. Then he was left on the line in the hot sun to drip and dry.

When the servant carried Tiger back to the dining hall he complained that either the tiger-skin rug was getting heavier or he was getting older and weaker.

That night the tiger did not eat any scraps, and he couldn't sleep. He knew that he would soon be found out and perhaps be made into a real tiger-skin rug. Whatever could he do?

Suddenly he heard a noise. All the hairs on his spine stood on end and the end of his tail twitched.

Three robbers were climbing in through the window.

They were carrying a sack and they began to fill it with silver dishes, ornaments and anything of value.

While Tiger was wondering what to do the door burst open and the Rajah rushed in.

The robbers knocked him down, and drew out wicked knives.

Then Tiger stood up and roared. The roar echoed down every corridor and round every room and across the palace gardens, waking everybody.

Tiger leapt to the

Rajah's rescue.

The three robbers took flight. They were in such a hurry that they became stuck in the window as they fought to get through all at once.

When the Rajah had recovered from his shock and his family and his servants had gathered, the Rajah proclaimed, 'The tiger-skin rug has saved us. He must stay for ever.'

And so he did.

He was never beaten and scrubbed again, but instead he bathed in the garden pool. He went on picnics with the family and rode on elephants. The children played with him and the Rajah's wives loved him.

He no longer ate scraps. He had his own plate of food and his own bowl of the best Indian tea.

In the evening he lay on the floor with the family around him, for he was still their tiger-skin rug – a real tiger-skin rug and the best in the whole world.

The End